Curlilocks
and the Big Bad
Hairbrush

TANGLED
PRESS

For my Aunties who lifted & loved me
For Riley, Benjamin, Lydia, Mo, Naome, Eitenne,Azana, &
the Klugh Men– I pass on the gift
YK

Summary: When Curlilocks delivers pies to her aunties, she finds each pie tempting. The Big Bad Hairbrush warns her about nibbling the Auntie's pies. Will she listen?

ISBN 0991027221
ISBN 978-0-9910272-2-4

Tangled Press
11824 Jollyville Rd, Suite 302
Austin, Texas 78759
www.TangledPress.com

TANGLED
— PRESS —

Curlilocks
and the Big Bad
Hairbrush

Once there was a little girl with super curly hair named Curlilocks. She lived with her family in a tiny town next to the Tallest Forest. Now, Curlilocks had a large family. There were lots of aunties, uncles, and cousins.

Friday was Auntie Day. That morning, Daddy baked a pie for each of Curlilocks's three aunties. Auntie Lizzie adored sweet potato pie, Auntie Birdie loved blackberry pie, and Auntie Adele fancied savory chicken pot pie.

"Curlilocks, here are the pies for your aunties. Savory or sweet, the aunties love their treats. Make sure to bring each auntie the whole pie," said Daddy.

Curlilocks plopped the pies into
her red wagon and packed her bag
with her favorite dream jar,
a butterfly net, and her hairbrush.

She and the little red wagon bounced along the path to Auntie Lizzie's. Curlilocks saw bright orange daisies growing around an old tree stump. Those orange daisies would be lovely next to the sweet potato pie. She picked the flowers and dropped them into the wagon.

As she got closer to Auntie Lizzie's pink house, she took a quick peek at the flowers and the sweet potato pie. Curlilocks was anxious to try just a tiny piece. Surely, a small morsel from the center would not be missed.

Curlilocks reached for the pie.
Suddenly she heard, "Savory or sweet,
the aunties love their treats;
but if you eat that pie, the aunties will
ask you why."

Curlilocks looked around and saw her hairbrush.
She answered,

"Oh please hush, you big bad hairbrush."

She quickly gobbled a tiny piece of pie and then knocked on Auntie Lizzie's door. "Here's your sweet potato pie, Auntie Lizzie," said Curlilocks. "Daddy made the whole pie just for you."

"Thank you," said Auntie Lizzie. She gave Curlilocks a hug and lifted the pie cover.

"Did someone gobble my pie?" asked Auntie Lizzie.

Curlilocks squeezed one eye shut, took a tiny breath, and whispered,

"**No.**"

Just as she said "no," her curly hair grew way bigger. Auntie Lizzie stared at Curlilock's hair and pondered her gobbled pie. She sent Curlilocks on to Auntie Birdie's house.

As she made her way to Auntie Birdie's house, Curlilocks found a curious rock. It looked like a tiny full moon. It was round and had brown dimples. She gently tucked the rock into her dream jar. The flat bottom and dimpled top of the moon rock reminded Curlilocks of Auntie Birdie's blackberry pie.

As she got closer to Auntie Birdie's blue house, she stopped to smell the blackberry pie. She thought about the sweet and tart blackberries. A small smidge would not be missed.

Curlilocks reached for the pie, when suddenly she heard, "Savory or sweet, the aunties love their treats; but if you eat that pie, the aunties will ask you why."

Curlilocks looked around, saw the hairbrush, and sighed. She answered,

"Oh please hush, you big bad hairbrush."

She nibbled a tiny piece of pie and then knocked on Auntie Birdie's door. "Here's your blackberry pie, Auntie Birdie," said Curlilocks. "Daddy made the whole pie just for you."

"Thank you, Curlilocks," said Auntie Birdie. She gave Curlilocks a hug and lifted the pie cover.

"Did someone nibble my pie?" asked Auntie Birdie.

Curlilocks squeezed one eye shut, took a tiny breath, and whispered,

"**No.**"

Just as she said "no," her curly hair grew way, way bigger. Auntie Birdie stared at Curlilock's hair and pondered the nibbled pie. She sent Curlilocks to Auntie Adele's house.

As she walked to Auntie Adele's yellow house, Curlilocks heard a buzzing noise. She looked up and found one sparkling, pale-blue dragonfly. He was flying up and down and side to side.

Curlilocks caught the dragonfly with her butterfly net. She let him out of the net, and he glided to the top of the pie cover. When Curlilocks shooed the dragonfly away, she could smell the pie spices.

Curlilocks peeked at Auntie Adele's pie. One little taste of crust would be yummy.

She reached for the pie, when suddenly she heard, "Savory or sweet, the aunties love their treats; but if you eat that pie, the aunties will ask you why."

Curlilocks looked around and saw the hairbrush again. She answered,

Oh please hush, you big bad hairbrush."

She plucked a tiny piece from the side and then knocked on Auntie Adele's door. "Here's your chicken pot pie, Auntie Adele," said Curlilocks. "Daddy made the whole pie just for you."

"Thank you, Curlilocks," said Auntie Adele. She gave Curlilocks a hug and lifted the pie cover.

Adele

Auntie Adele peeked at the pie and then at Curlilocks. "Did someone pluck a piece of my pie?" asked Auntie Adele.

Curlilocks squeezed one eye shut, took a tiny breath, and whispered,

"NO."

Just as she said "no," her curly hair grew way, way, way bigger.

Auntie Adele stared and said, "Curlilocks, telling me the truth will not get you into trouble. When you want to share, it's good to ask."

"Okay," Curlilocks said, relieved. "Auntie Adele, I gobbled a piece of Auntie Lizzie's sweet potato pie, nibbled a bit of Auntie Birdie's blackberry pie, and plucked a piece of your chicken pot pie."

Suddenly, her way, way, way bigger hair shrunk neatly back into place. Auntie Adele gave Curlilocks a hug and called the other aunties over for dinner. They set out a picnic and watched the dragonflies dash around while they ate the sweet potato pie, blackberry pie, and savory chicken pot pie.

Big Bad Hairbrush Word List

Savory—spicy or salty, without being sweet

Morsel—a bite, mouthful, or small piece of food

Curious—strange, unusual, or unexpected

Tart—a sharp or sour taste

Ponder—think about something carefully

Visit us at www.TangledPress.com

CPSIA information can be obtained
at www.ICGtesting.com
Printed in the USA
LVHW072024160719
624280LV00005B/122/P